Dear Parent:
Your child's love of reading starts here!

Every child learns to read in a different way and at his or her own speed. Some go back and forth between reading levels and read favorite books again and again. Others read through each level in order. You can help your young reader improve and become more confident by encouraging his or her own interests and abilities. From books your child reads with you to the first books he or she reads alone, there are I Can Read Books for every stage of reading:

SHARED READING
Basic language, word repetition, and whimsical illustrations, ideal for sharing with your emergent reader

BEGINNING READING
Short sentences, familiar words, and simple concepts for children eager to read on their own

READING WITH HELP
Engaging stories, longer sentences, and language play for developing readers

READING ALONE
Complex plots, challenging vocabulary, and high-interest topics for the independent reader

I Can Read Books have introduced children to the joy of reading since 1957. Featuring award-winning authors and illustrators and a fabulous cast of beloved characters, I Can Read Books set the standard for beginning readers.

A lifetime of discovery begins with the magical words **"I Can Read!"**

Visit www.icanread.com for information
on enriching your child's reading experience.

To Grandad Riley and the old rusted car by the pond
that we pretended to drive, and to Daddy
and trips to the farm
—J.D.R.

For our Awesome Austin-man. Always a-smilin'
—B.D.

I Can Read Book® is a trademark of HarperCollins Publishers.

Adobe Photoshop® was used to prepare the full-color art.
Axel the Truck: Field Trip! Copyright © 2014, 2019 by HarperCollins Publishers. All rights reserved. No part of this book may be used or reproduced in any manner whatsoever without written permission except in the case of brief quotations embodied in critical articles and reviews. Manufactured in China. For information address HarperCollins Children's Books, a division of HarperCollins Publishers, 195 Broadway, New York, NY 10007.
www.icanread.com

Library of Congress Control Number: 2018949826
ISBN 978-0-06-269281-8 (hardback)—ISBN 978-0-06-269280-1 (pbk. ed.)

19 20 21 22 23   SCP   10 9 8 7 6 5 4 3 2 1   ❖   First Edition

 Greenwillow Books

My First I Can Read!

SHARED READING

Axel

THE TRUCK

Field Trip

Story by **J. D. Riley**

Pictures by **Brandon Dorman**

Greenwillow Books, *An Imprint of HarperCollins Publishers*

Axel is a red truck.

Axel has big, big wheels.

"I like to go fast," Axel says.
Vroom, vroom, varoom!
Axel speeds down the road.

Axel's big tires zoom around.

Zip, zip, zoom.

Axel heads to the farm.

"Great dirt road!" Axel says.

Dust swirls under his tires.

Swish, whish, whoosh!

Bugs splat on his windshield.
Ping, zing, splat!
"Bugs and dust rule!" Axel says.

Axel races off the road.

Axel rolls across the fields.

Rumble, rumble, thump.

Weeds catch in his bumper.

Clip, clip, clump.

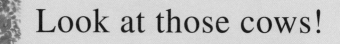

Look at those cows!

The cows run after Axel.

Moove, moove, moove.

Axel sees the pond—too late!
Glush, glush, glush.

Axel the truck is stuck.

He rocks his tires,
back and forth.
Blump, brump, boing.

He revs his engine.

Vroom, vroom, varoom.

He shifts gears.

Grrr, grrr, grrr.

Axel is free!

Axel zooms home.

Axel is covered with bugs
and mud and muck.

"Yahoo!" yells Axel.

"That was monster fun!"